MIGHTY MORPHIN

POWER RANGERS

THE MOVIE

™

PHOTO STORYBOOK

First published in Great Britain in 1995
by Mammoth, an imprint of Reed Children's Books
Michelin House, 81 Fulham Road, London SW3 6RB
and Auckland, Melbourne, Singapore and Toronto
TM and © 1995 Saban Entertainment, Inc. and Saban International N.V.
Mighty Morphin Power Rangers and all logos, character names and
distinctive likenesses thereof are trademarks of
Saban Entertainment, Inc. and Saban International N.V.

Ivan Ooze, Oozemen, Tengu and Dulcea TM and © 1995 Twentieth Century Fox Film Corporations

Book design by Barbara Zuniga
Copyright © 1995 Reed International Books Ltd

ISBN 0-7497-2056-5

Printed in the UK by Cambus Litho Ltd

Long ago and far away, a legendary inter-dimensional being, known as Zordon, came to the city of Angel Grove to establish a vanguard to spearhead the never-ending struggle against evil. With the aid of his trusted assistant, Alpha 5, the noble master sought out six extraordinary teenagers and gave them the power to transform into a superhuman fighting force. In time of great need, the young heroes could now call upon colossal assault vehicles known as "Zords". While the identity of the six remained a guarded secret, their courageous exploits soon became the stuff of legend, earning them the title:

THE MIGHTY MORPHIN POWER RANGERS.

It seemed like just another afternoon in Angel Grove, until some builders dug up a whole lot of trouble! Their digging disturbed a secret chamber – the hiding place for a mysterious, giant, stone egg.

"Let's see if there's a yolk in there," joked the foreman, giving the egg a crack with his hammer. **KZAAAAP!** A bolt of purple lightning sent him flying through the air.

The police were called and arrived to cordon off the area.

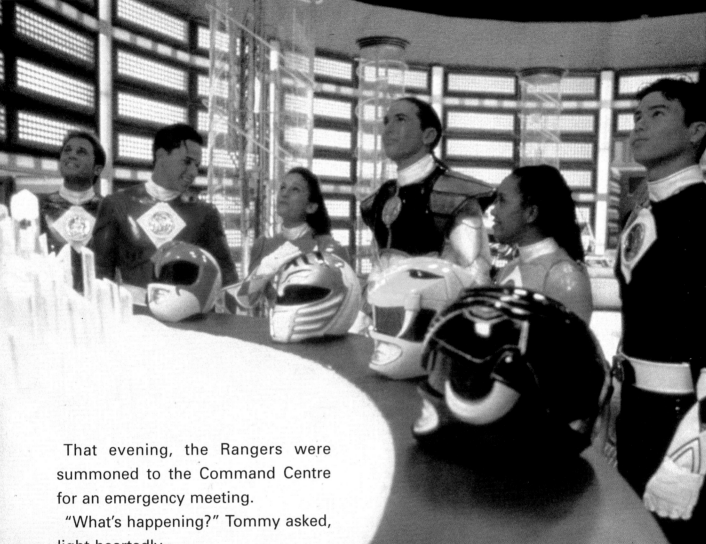

That evening, the Rangers were summoned to the Command Centre for an emergency meeting.

"What's happening?" Tommy asked, light-heartedly.

Zordon looked stern. "Rangers," he replied, "you must act swiftly. The planet is in grave danger!"

"Danger from what?" puzzled Kimberly.

"Six thousand years ago," Zordon continued, "Ivan Ooze, a being evil beyond all understanding, was finally captured and placed in a hyperlock chamber, deep under the ground. But now the chamber has been disturbed. You must return it to the depths of the earth before it is opened and Ivan is released!"

Unfortunately, the evil secrets of the awesome egg were known by two others – the Mistress of Mayhem herself, Rita Repulsa and the wicked warrior, Lord Zedd!

"At last," Zedd shouted, "after two thousand years of searching, I have finally found you!" One blast from his staff was enough to open the egg with a horrible hiss, and reveal a bubbling, belching yolk of purple ooze.

"Two thousand years for this tub of

snot?" Rita Repulsa laughed.

But as she spoke, a hideous transformation was taking place. The ooze spluttered, boiled and frothed into the ghastly form of Ivan Ooze.

"Ladies and Gentlemen . . . the Ooze is back!" Ivan announced, oozing charm.

Lord Zedd grovelled. "It is a supreme honour to finally meet you," he said. "All I ask is that you might help me to destroy Zordon, forever."

"I will not only destroy him," hissed Ivan in reply, "I will obliterate his entire legacy. It will be like Zordon of Eltare never existed!"

Shafts of coloured light lit up the night sky as the Rangers arrived to find only an empty egg and a puzzled-looking security guard.

"You haven't seen a morphological being lurking round here?" Kimberly asked the patrol man.

"You mean, like this!" exclaimed the guard as his body stretched into the terrifying shape of Ooze. "Allow me to introduce myself: I am the despicable Ivan Ooze!"

"And we're the Mighty Morphin Power Rangers," Tommy cut in, "so you might as well pack your bags, raisin-head!"

"Oooh! What a big mouth!" mocked Ivan. "Let's see how you like it when it's full of SLIME!"

With a snap of his fingers he was gone – in his place appeared a dozen Ooze Men, more terrifying than any of Rita's Putty Patrol.

"Let's take these slimeballs!" shouted Adam. The Rangers went to work with all their best moves as fists and feet flew in all directions. Kimberly used a plank as a see-saw and sent one of the creatures flying. Tommy tripped-up two of them with a spade handle. But the Ooze Men were fast, and soon matched the Rangers move for move. Aisha and Adam struggled bravely, but morphing was the only

way out. KAZAM! A blinding golden light engulfed the superheroes as they were transformed into complete Power Rangers. The creatures seemed to have vanished into the night, but it wasn't long before the Rangers found the Ooze Men and defeated them.

The battle was over, for now. But something was wrong – the Rangers' uniforms suddenly dematerialized and none of their communicators would work. By the time they had walked back to the Command Centre, it was too late – Ivan Ooze had got there first and destroyed the HQ. Zordon lay amongst the smoking ruins looking very ill and old.

"What's happening to him?" Aisha asked, tearfully.

"Outside of his time warp he's ageing at a vastly accelerated rate!" Billy explained. "We have to get him back inside, and quick."

Zordon opened his eyes. "I'm afraid that's impossible," he murmured. "The Power has been destroyed. The Power Rangers are no more." It all looked hopeless.

Alpha 5 had an idea. "I have heard tales of another power," he said. "It is watched over by the Master Warrior of the Planet Phaedos."

"How can we get there?" Tommy asked.

Alpha 5 shook his head. "It's far too dangerous. I have just enough power to get you there, but not to bring you back."

"Then we'll just have to hope that the legend is true," Kimberly cut in. "Zordon's life depends on us."

Reluctantly, Alpha 5 programmed the transporter co-ordinates. "May you reach the Great Power!" he shouted, pulling the control lever. The Rangers disappeared into the ether on the start of their greatest adventure.

Phaedos seemed a hot and barren planet. The Rangers had landed safely in the middle of a deserted, rocky wasteland. They saw no sign of life, until Aisha discovered a hideous decomposed creature with a spear in its side.

"What was it?" asked Billy.

"Not the welcoming committee, that's for sure!" Kimberly replied.

Tommy led the way as they trekked across the desolate plain – all the Rangers were on their guard.

Suddenly, they were startled by a blood-curdling screech. From out of the sky, silhouetted against the burning sun, came ten ferocious, giant birds – Tengu Warriors sent by Ivan Ooze.

Their claws and beaks ripped at the powerless Rangers, now just ordinary teenagers. There was nowhere to hide. It looked as if they would never see Angel Grove again, after all.

Then a cry went up. From high in the rocks came a wild and beautiful warrior woman, her hands expertly spinning two sticks which whined and whistled and drove the Tengu mad. They covered their ears, then flew off as fast as they could.

Tommy advanced to thank the extraordinary soldier. But before he could open his mouth she had tripped him with her spear, pinning him to the ground with its point.

"Leave Phaedos . . . before it's too late!" she snarled.

Aisha stepped forward. "We don't want any trouble," she faltered, "our leader Zordon –"

The Amazonian warrior looked startled. "Did you say Zordon?" she demanded.

"You know Zordon?" Kimberly asked, incredulously. "Who are you?"

"I am Dulcea," she said, releasing Tommy, "Master Warrior of the Planet Phaedos."

"Then you're the one who is supposed to help us destroy Ivan Ooze!" Rocky piped up.

"Ivan Ooze is free?" Dulcea looked shocked. "He is a monster. If we don't hurry then your planet is doomed. Now, follow me."

Meanwhile, in Angel Grove, Ivan Ooze had taken over the local chemical plant. His evil plan was to manufacture gallons of his noxious ooze, then make an army of all the local children and turn their parents into zombies.

The next day, Ivan held a huge party in Angel Grove Park – all the children were invited, and all the ooze was free. Ivan had changed his shape into a friendly looking Wizard.

"Guys and girls, girls and guys, gather round and feast your eyes," he sang, as the children danced joyfully around him. "I promise you all you just can't lose with your own supply of Ivan's Ooze."

The children went wild and started throwing ooze at each other. Ivan's plan was starting to work. He sang another verse:

"Come one, come all,
To the ooze free-for-all!
Take it home in boxes,
Take it home in cases,
If your parents try to stop you,
Then just throw it in their faces!"

His words whipped the children into a frenzy; soon his juvenile army would be ready to cause mayhem.

It had been a long journey for the Rangers. On the way, Dulcea had told them of terrible Ivan's reign of terror, thousands of years before; of how Zordon had saved them all; and of how she owed Zordon her life.

They had arrived at a mountain plateau which overlooked the dense forest below. There, rising majestically from the centre of the woodland was a huge, stone monolith – the source of the Power of the Universe.

"The monolith is heavily guarded against intruders," warned Dulcea. "No one has ever entered there and lived to tell the tale." The Rangers looked downcast. "But you were chosen by Zordon, and I have faith in his wisdom," she continued. "We will call upon the sacred animals of the Ninjetti for help." She scooped up a handful of sand and gently blew it

into a raging bonfire.

Suddenly, the Rangers found themselves transformed into Ninjas, each of them with a new animal emblem. Tommy was the Falcon; Aisha, the Bear; Rocky, the mighty Ape; Billy, the Wolf; Kimberly, the Crane; and Adam, the Frog!

At last, the Rangers had some of their powers back, and now it was time for Dulcea to bid them a sad farewell as she couldn't leave the plateau without ageing rapidly and losing her powers. "To those who know the Ninjetti," she told them, "anything is possible. The strength is inside you. Trust it. Your sacred animals will be your guide."

With that, and a swift "goodbye", Dulcea was gone – transformed into an owl, she flew off into the distance, leaving the Rangers amazed.

Something astonishing had happened in Angel Grove. The ooze had infected all the grown-ups and turned them into zombies! Hundreds of parents left their homes and marched down the street to the wicked Ooze's factory.

Nothing could disturb them – it was as if they were sleepwalking. Ivan Ooze had a willing band of slaves who would follow his every command.

Some of them were put to work in the chemical plant, the rest were taken to the building site. Ivan and Goldar decided to have a bit of fun.

"Simon says . . . bow to your leader!" Ivan commanded. The adults bowed, frantically.

"Simon says . . . "

"Quack like a duck!" Goldar interjected.

The grown-ups quacked, crazily – the noise was too much for Ivan.

"Shut up, shut up!" he yelled. But still the noise went on.

"You didn't say, 'Simon says'," Goldar volunteered.

in a trance and digging furiously, just like all the other parents.

Ivan Ooze arrived at the site. He was delighted to see that the parents had already uncovered a huge mechanical arm and leg. "Feast your eyes upon the skeleton of the barbaric Hornitor!" he shouted. "The dreadful Scorpitron should be close by," he continued, dribbling with excitement. "Once my terrible Ecto-Morphicon machines are up and running, I shall annihilate Angel Grove, and then . . .

THE UNIVERSE!"

Fred ran away as fast as he could. Ivan Ooze must be stopped, but how?

The next day, Ivan had another children's party in the park. By now, all the children had been hypnotised by him, except for young Fred Kelman who resisted his powers. "I've got to find my Dad," he thought, "he'll know what to do."

But when Fred got to the building site, he found his father

The Rangers started to make their way carefully through the forest when they strayed into an animal graveyard. A dinosaur skeleton attacked – but Tommy dislodged a bone and the creature fell apart like a house of cards. When they reached the forest's clearing they approached the monolith. Menacing carved gargoyles looked down on them.

Suddenly, Kimberly screamed. The gargoyles had come alive!

In a flash, the Rangers were transformed into Ninjetti. They fought bravely against their toughest foes yet, but would their Ninjetti powers alone be enough against the fearsome guardians of the Ultimate Power? After a desperate struggle, Adam helped Rocky send a vicious gargoyle plunging into the river far below. Kimberly and Tommy took out another as they tipped a massive boulder to smash one of the creatures over the cliff. Adam was in deep trouble again – trapped between two axe-wielding gargoyles; but Billy yanked him to safety on the end of a rope, and the two gargoyles crashed into each other, exploding into a thousand pieces.

Finally, the Rangers united to turn on the last gargoyle. One final bullet-dive from Tommy smashed the devilish creature into the wall of the monolith where it crumbled into dust.

The doorway rumbled open to reveal a shaft of dazzling white light from which a gigantic, ancient pyramid emerged. A huge crystal seal dominated its face, together with the images of the six sacred animals that the Rangers now represented.

Instinctively, they knew what to do next: "I am the Wolf!" chanted Billy.

"The Crane!" said Kimberly.

"The Bear!" said Aisha.

"The Frog!" cried Adam.

"The Ape!" said Rocky.

"The Falcon!" Tommy concluded.

The crystal seal burned brighter and brighter. Heavenly music filled the air as the six animal spirits momentarily came to life and swirled around them like ghostly Zords. With a blinding snap of light which left them glowing, the young heroes found that their soft Ninja suits had been converted into the hard body-armour of complete Power Rangers.

"We have the POWER!" yelled Tommy with delight.

"Hang on, Angel Grove!" Adam exclaimed, "We're on our way!"

Angel Grove had been wrecked. Ivan Ooze had finally unleashed his evil Ecto-Morphicons, Scorpitron and Hornitor to blaze a trail of destruction through the town.

Fred knew he had to persuade his friends that their parents were in danger. He found them in Ernie's Snack Bar having a wild ooze party.

"Ivan Ooze isn't your friend – he's using all of us, and our parents to take over the planet!" Fred urged. With that they set off for the building site to find their parents.

Six streaks of colour lit up the night sky above Angel Grove. Ivan Ooze looked up for a moment. "I smell. . . Power Rangers!" he said with disgust.

The six superheroes were astonished by the mess that Ooze and his monsters had created. "Ivan's going to pay for this!" said Rocky.

"Big time!" agreed Adam.

There was no time to lose. Scorpitron was thumping down the street ahead of them and blasting every car in its path. Behind them, the Rangers could hear the terrifying shriek of the Hornitor approaching. They watched in horror as it arrogantly ripped out a lamp post.

"This could be a long night," joked Billy. "We need Zord power!"

"Then let's do it!" yelled Tommy.

The Rangers clicked their new power coins into their morphers. A globe of light shot up into the sky, then erupted with a crackle of morphin energy. From out of the globe burst the six new Ninja Zords – the Falcon, the Wolf, the Ape, the Frog, the Crane and the Bear. The Mighty Morphin machines swooped over Angel Grove Tower, truly a sight to behold.

The Rangers were soon on board their Ninja Zords and experimenting with the new controls.

"Check out the astro-navigation modulars!" exclaimed Billy.

"And the ten disc CD-player!" laughed Kimberly.

Tommy was first into Battle Mode. He turned the Falcon Ninja Zord towards Scorpitron and put the machine into a steep dive. The Ecto-Morphicon was in his sights. "Rockets deployed!" he announced. The battle for Angel Grove had begun.

Blam! Blam! Falcon Ninja Zord's missiles whistled past Scorpitron and exploded harmlessly in the street. Scorpitron responded with laser blasts which winged the Falcon.

"I've been hit!" yelled Tommy. As he pulled out, Adam's Frog Ninja Zord joined the fight. It lashed out its huge metallic tongue and coiled it around the Scorpitron's throat. Scorpitron struggled to break free, dragging the mighty amphibian with it.

Elsewhere, the buildings shook as a savage struggle took place between Hornitor and the brutal Bear Ninja Zord.

Kimberly's Crane Ninja Zord had locked onto Ivan Ooze

in Angel Grove Tower and was preparing to dive.

But the Ooze man was ready.

"Well, if it isn't that cute little pink Ranger," he oozed, pointing at the Crane. Shazam! A bolt of energy left his finger and wrapped itself around Kimberly's machine. The Crane Ninja Zord had been frozen by a pulsating electro-plasmic lasso!

The Scorpitron meanwhile, was in trouble. The giant fangs of Billy's Wolf Ninja Zord had clamped onto the Ecto-morphicon's tail, and Billy clung on for dear life.

Ivan was continuing to sizzle Kimberly in the Crane Ninja Zord cockpit. As she frantically punched at the control panels, she accidentally hit a bank of buttons, and with a surge of supersonic speed broke free from Ivan's magical grip.

The Wolf Ninja Zord had tightened his grip, and bit harder and harder until Scorpitron's tail sheared off and whipped across the street. Gallons of Ooze poured out from the evil Ecto-Morphicon, who shrieked wildly. Then, as the Frog Ninja Zord released its choking grip – BOOM! BOOM! From out of nowhere, two missiles found their target and turned the beleaguered beast into a fireball.

"Falcon Ninja Zord is back in the game!" announced Tommy, swooping past. "All right, Tommy!" yelled Adam. "One down, one to go."

KAPOOWWW!

Meanwhile, Hornitor was angry. He had swiped the Bear Ninja Zord away, to be replaced by Rocky's Ape Ninja Zord. They wrestled furiously for a while, but the Hornitor finally sent the mighty Ape hurtling down the street, halting at the feet of Aisha's Bear. Adam's Frog

Ninja Zord was soon on the scene with the Wolf Ninja Zord close behind. Above them, the Falcon Ninja Zord and Kimberly's Crane Ninja Zord hovered in readiness. Hornitor's spirit sank and he turned to run.

Ivan Ooze roared furiously. "They've destroyed my beautiful creation. They're going to pay for this!"

Ivan stretched out his body like a huge piece of gum. He burst through the Hornitor's back which swelled to create a revolting hybrid, as tall as Angel Grove Tower, only much, much scarier.

"We need Ninja Megazord Power, now!" ordered Tommy. Within moments, the Zords were transformed into the menacing Ninja Megazord. Tommy stood by in the Falcon Ninja Zord ready to attack from behind. Ivan Hornitor strode towards them, smashing through the monorail track on his way. He

The train shot over the back of the Falcon to safety.

But things weren't going so smoothly for the other Rangers. Ivan Hornitor zapped the groggy Ninja Megazord with a blast of crackling energy, destroying the back-up systems. Then, he hurled the great Zord through the roof of the Angel Grove First National Bank, where it lay powerless in the rubble.

The Hornitor towered above the ruins, his arms raised in triumph.

"End of the road, kiddies!" he laughed.

ripped up the Angel Grove Tower to use as a club. The Ninja Megazord responded by activating its Power Sword and taking up fighting stance.

The Hornitor hit home with a baseball stroke that stunned the Ninja Megazord, crashing its control systems.

"Tommy, we need your help!" called Kimberly.

But Tommy could see a train heading straight for the broken monorail track.

"I'll be there as soon as I can," he replied as he powered downwards.

He glided into position, the wings bridging the broken rails just in time.

BLAM!

Blam! Blam! Tommy sent Hornitor spinning with two rocket blasts.

"Falcon Ninja Zord coming in!" radioed Tommy. The last Zord locked into position and with a crackle of energy, the all-powerful Ninja Megafalcon Zord rose majestically.

Now in the Ninja Megafalcon Zord cockpit, Tommy steered the craft into the sky.

"I'm setting course for outer space," Billy announced. "I think I know how we can finish the job," he said mysteriously.

Ivan Hornitor took off in pursuit and tackled the Zord to send the two of them spinning off into space.

"We have to get back on course," said Billy. The mighty Zord palmed Ivan away and escaped. "Bearing 008144," Billy continued as the Ninja

YEEEEOOOWWW!

Megafalcon Zord headed for the stars. Finally, Billy brought their fantastic craft to a halt. The Zord, now in Battle Mode, was ready for the final attack.

"It's almost time," Billy announced, mysteriously.

"Time for what?" asked Adam.

"Ryan's Comet, of course!" exclaimed Billy. He explained his plan. "We get Ivan into the comet's path . . ."

". . . And Kaboom! He's space dust!" Aisha continued.

"Brace yourselves!" yelled Tommy.

Hornitor shoulder-charged them and sparks flew as the grappling giants tumbled right into the comet's path.

With only seconds to go until impact there seemed to be no escape. At least it would be the end for Ivan Hornitor, as well.

But Aisha hadn't given up. She had found a switch marked 'FOR EMERGENCY USE ONLY'.

"Desperate times call for desperate measures!"she exclaimed, flicking the switch. ZAP! The Ninja Megafalcon Zord walloped Ivan with a lightning knee-kick to the midriff.

"YEEEEOOOWWW!" screamed Ivan Hornitor, bending double in pain.

"We're outta here!" Tommy rejoiced. The Zord sped off as Hornitor spun helplessly towards the comet.

KAAABOOOM! It was as if Ivan Ooze had never existed as a billion flaming particles showered every corner of the universe. The supreme silence of space had regained control.

KAAABOOM!

When the Mighty Morphins arrived back at the Command Centre, Alpha 5 looked sad.

"Rangers . . . " he murmured, "I'm afraid you are too late." Zordon's old and lifeless form lay peacefully before them.

Everyone was stunned. But then Tommy remembered something.

"Wait," he said. "Remember Zordon's words. 'To those who possess the Great Power, all things are possible.'"

The Rangers joined hands and formed a circle around Zordon. As they bowed their heads, a shimmering energy flowed out of their bodies and into Zordon. A dazzling explosion followed. When the smoke cleared, the Command Centre was back to normal again and a youthful Zordon looked down from his pillar of light.

"Zordon!" chorused the excited Morphins.

"Rangers!" replied Zordon, with a fierce pride. "It's good to see you, again. Once more I shall be able to look down on you and guide you."

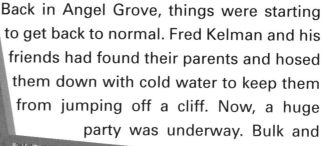

Back in Angel Grove, things were starting to get back to normal. Fred Kelman and his friends had found their parents and hosed them down with cold water to keep them from jumping off a cliff. Now, a huge party was underway. Bulk and

Skull were bragging as usual, but no one wanted to listen.

"Look who's here," said Rocky, as he greeted Fred.

"I hear you were quite the hero," said Kimberly. Fred blushed. "I just helped a little," he said, shyly. "The Rangers are the real heroes."

"Just helped?" asked Aisha. "I hear you could be in line to be a Ranger yourself, before too long."

"Anything's possible," said Tommy.

"You really think so?" Fred asked.

"Hey," Tommy replied, with quiet confidence, "I know so."

Fireworks shot into the air and Angel Grove Bridge came alive with lights proclaiming:

"THANK YOU, POWER RANGERS!"

The party was still in full swing as a proud father and son walked home.

"Fred Kelman, the Gold Ranger," the boy yawned. "It does have a certain ring to it!"